MR. DELA ROSA

-Presents-

Sex With Celebrities: Volume 1

In order of appearance

Emma Watson
Kate Upton
Halle Berry
Jessica Alba
Jennifer Aniston
Kim Kardashian
Sofia Vergara
Megan Fox

Emma Watson

The night air was cold and her skin was luxuriously warm as she pressed herself against me, wrapping her arms around my neck and kissing passionately. I could feel her hot breath as our tongues touched and explored. My heart was pounding in my chest. *Could I be so lucky?* I had never been a lucky guy before. Was tonight the night for me? Was all of my lifelong karma finally coming through on its promise? Either way, as Emma lifted one leg and wrapped it around my waist, I knew that it was actually happening. Thousands of men and boys around the world would be falling asleep tonight and dreaming about a passionate night with Emma Watson. I would be living it.

She was wearing only a skimpy little party dress, despite the cold, along with her black heels and simple jewellery. I could still see her in my mind's eye, dancing to the latina music that the new club down on Main Street specialized in. I hadn't even noticed it at first, when I bumped into her. Then, before I knew it, we had made the first, fleeting eye contact and then we were dancing next to each other. Dancing *against* each other. Now, we were outside in the cold night air and she was running her hands through my hair with her leg wrapped tightly around me. She was hot to trot and I was the man she had chosen. I ran my hand along her leg and marveled at how warm and smooth she felt. She was a truly luxurious young woman. I could feel her breasts pushing against my chest and I had one arm wrapped around her narrow waist, pressing her harder against me. I moved away from her tongue and kissed her neck and her earlobes, breathing against her ear and exploring further down her waist with my hands.

Emma moaned in my ear as I touched her. My dick was throbbing inside my pants as I pressed it against her, aching to be inside this gorgeous woman. I had never been so hard.

I needed to get her to a room; fast.

"Do you live close by?" I breathed in her ear, grabbing her waist and pulling her harder against me. She responded by squeezing her leg harder. She wanted it just as much as I did and I knew that she could feel my bulging manhood pressed against her.

Emma shook her head. "My driver will be looking for me soon," she whispered. That British accent was unbelievably sexy.

She had a driver?

Uh-oh. That was bad news.

My place was a half-hour taxi fare away and there was no guarantee my housemates wouldn't be home by the time we got there. I pictured our dirty laundry on the floor and my unmade bed, with my x-box controllers still there where I had left them next to the pillows. My place was not the place to take Emma Watson – movie star and goddess in human form. Half an hour was too far. What if her lust petered away by then? What if her driver kicked up a fuss and she decided it wasn't worth it? No, if this was my only chance to have Emma Watson on my dick, I wasn't going to take any chances.

"What's wrong with here?" I suggested, still working my hands along her legs and feeling her arse. God, she felt amazing.

Emma didn't even open her eyes to look around. "Wherever," she moaned, gyrating her hips against me and leaning her head back. I pressed my face into her exposed cleavage and kissed and licked her skin, more eager than ever to have her naked before me. The night air was cold, but our skin was hot to touch and the alcohol was coursing through our veins. Here would be fine.

We were in the middle of a park, lit sporadically by old-fashioned street lamps. So far as I could tell, it was vacant, except for us. The sun was only a couple of hours away and most people would be at home sleeping now. I was confident that we wouldn't be disturbed, although I didn't really care, either. If the paparazzi caught us, perhaps I would become famous in my own right? The Australian exchange student who fucked Emma Watson in a park. I would've laughed at the thought had I not been preoccupied with Emma's perfect, firm tits. I picked her up and she wrapped her legs around me whilst I carried her further onto the grass. There was a bench seat nearby, but the grass looked far more inviting. I lowered her gently onto the grass and lay on top of her, thrusting incessantly and grinding myself against her pussy. She moaned and closed her eyes again. The look of pleasure on her face almost had me cumming already. She didn't seem to mind the grass.

Green light.

I pulled the straps down off her shoulders and almost snapped her bra in my eagerness to get her tits out as I undid it and pulled all the straps off her arms. Her boobs were bared in front of me and my hands were there in an instant, feeling them and delighting in how soft and delicate and *warm* she was. Emma was incredibly feminine. I wanted more. I reached up her dress and had her knickers down and off her feet. Now, her pussy was exposed and her legs were spread wide open for me. I kissed and licked down the inside of her thigh and Emma's breathing quickened as I drew closer and closer. Finally, I licked her pussy and worked my tongue around her clit. Emma groaned, almost so loud as to worry me that someone nearby might hear her. She arched her back and I felt her fingers running through my hair.

I continued to lick her pussy.

Suddenly, Emma had her legs across my back and, before I knew it, she had rolled me over and was sitting on my chest. *Was that some kind of celebrity martial arts move? How did she do that?* I could feel her wet pussy, dripping wet and touching my shirt. Evidently, she didn't mind returning the star treatment. She smiled at me and then came close and kissed my neck. She worked her hands up the front of my shirt and pulled it over my head. Then, smiling tantalizingly at me and even giggling occasionally, she kissed her way down my front whilst her hands tugged at my waist band and worked my fly. The cold air touched my dick and I gasped as she pulled it free and pushed my pants further down my legs. She didn't stop at my navel, kissing and licking until; finally, Emma Watson flicked her hair back, held my dick firmly in her hand and guided it into the warmth and perfect wetness of her mouth.

I couldn't prevent the voice from screaming in my head. *Emma Watson is sucking my dick!* And wow, she had obviously done this before. She sucked me beautifully, flicking her big brown eyes up to me every so often to see how her work was being received. I held her by her hair and lay my head back in the grass, enjoying the moment. After a few moments, Emma was straddling me again, with her knees on the grass. She smiled and giggled at me a little nervously as she felt for my dick. Obviously, she wasn't concerned about wearing a condom. She held my dick upright and, slowly, with a look of feminine pleasure on her face, Emma lowered herself onto my dick. She squealed slightly as I entered her fully and I couldn't help but gasp.

"*Godddd*," Emma groaned.

Her mouth had felt amazing wrapped around my dick, but her pussy was even better. She was truly a goddess. She was unbelievably tight, warm and wet and she got straight into it, working her hips and riding my cock, right there on the grass in the middle of the park.

The view from my perspective was the stuff of dreams. Emma Watson was gasping with each thrust and her hair and boobs were bouncing in front of my face.

I decided to assert my authority and I rolled her back over. I wanted to dominate this woman. This beauty. With her soft legs wrapped around me and still wearing her heels, I fucked her hard, watching her boobs bouncing and feeling her body moving under me. She moaned even louder now and put her hands up to cover her own mouth. I was slamming her and she was loving it.

I pulled one of her legs across and had her on her hands and knees in front of me. I took a moment to relish the view and take photos with my mind. Emma Watson was on her hands and knees in front of me and her body looked just breath-taking in its perfection. I grabbed her hips and maneuvered my dick into her tight pussy again. I pulled her hair and slapped her arse and fucked her hard and she moaned and squealed until finally, I pulled out and finished on her back. I groaned as I came on her. My knees went weak from the power of the orgasm. I could think of nothing else but the beauty that was Emma Watson laid out in front of me, taking my cum on her back like a good girl.

"Whoa," I groaned and fell back onto the grass, panting.

Emma slumped on the ground next to me and I heard her moaning softly for a while. Then, she rolled over and started squirming awkwardly, cleaning herself on the grass. "You got it everywhere," she exclaimed, not completely unhappy about that.

I could only nod in agreement. I was trying to commit this entire experience to memory.

I lay there in the cold night air, whilst Emma's phone suddenly started ringing. She didn't answer it, but she got to work on putting her bra and her dress back where they belonged. Suddenly, without so much as a goodbye, Emma Watson was off and walking away, disappearing into the darkness in the direction of the club that we had started at. I watched after her, enjoying the view of her swaying hips and the knowledge that I had just dominated her. I lay there a while longer and stared up at the stars. Slowly, I got around to pulling my pants back up and putting my shirt back on.

There was no way anybody would ever believe me when I told them what I had done tonight. That didn't matter, I decided. This would be a night and a fuck that I would never forget.

Kate Upton

The sun was shining overhead and the waves were crashing. It had been a good session out in the waves. I had my own secret headland break with a tiny, secluded beach. It took half an hour to hike to it and there were no paths through the trees. My own little piece of paradise.

I caught my final wave and rode it as far in as it could take me. I didn't even notice her until I was up on the sand with my board under my arm. There was a woman on my beach and she was sunbathing. Evidently, she didn't much enjoy tan lines, because she was topless. I was a little disgruntled at first. This was supposed to be my little secret! But oh well, what did it really matter? At least there weren't crowds flocking here. I had to walk past the topless woman to get back into the trees and head back to my car. She had her eyes shut and seemed completely oblivious to my presence. I tried my best to be polite and not look at her as I passed by.

"Oh!" the woman must have noticed me for she suddenly sat bolt upright and covered herself with her hands.

"Don't mind me," I said, patting the air reassuringly.

She just sat there and watched me pass by. I had almost walked right past her when the light bulb went off and I came to an abrupt halt. *Surely, my eyes must be deceiving me.*

"Ah," I turned awkwardly to face the woman again. *Yep, it was definitely her!* "You're not Kate Upton by any chance, are you?" I asked, knowing the answer full well. "The model?"

"Do you want an autograph?" she asked bitingly. "I thought this beach was private."

I shrugged. "I thought so, too," I said. "I've been coming here for years. First time I've ever seen anyone else."

"No one else knows about it?" Kate asked. "Just you?"

"And you, it seems," I said. "Don't like tan lines, huh?"

That got a little smile and I saw her relax a little. My heart beat a little faster. I'd been with models before. I knew that I could catch their eye, but Kate Upton? She was another story altogether, surely. Still, I saw her eyes flitting up and down my body and I wondered what she saw. Tall surfer guy with muscles and a tan? I kept in good shape. Just maybe…

Then, Kate relaxed entirely and she let her hands fall away.

I caught my breath. I had seen photos of her in bikini shots and runway shots before, but in reality, her boobs were completely out of this world! Big, perfectly shaped and perky, she was a goddess in the flesh and she was topless in front of me.

"Yep, you're definitely Kate Upton," I observed, nodding my approval. "Nice to meet you." I took a chance and stuck my board in the sand and extended my hand to her. She reached out and took it and I couldn't stop myself from staring at her bare breasts. Perfection!

We sat in the sun and chatted for a while, listening to the waves and enjoying the feeling of the breeze on our skin and the sand between our toes. She wasn't shy at all. My eyes continually flicked towards her body.

It wasn't long before I was pulling her towards me and kissing her.

She rolled on top of me and straddled my lap, with her tits out right in front of my face in all their glory. I ran my fingers up the side of her legs and along the side of her stomach until finally; I felt her boobs in my hands. They were full, firm, soft and they were huge! My cock was rock hard in my board shorts now and Kate rubbed herself against it, still kissing and exploring each other with our hands.

I felt Kate's hands tugging at the string that tied my shorts. She was clearly wasting no time. She knew what she wanted and she wasn't shy about it either. Before I even had time to comprehend what was happening, Kate Upton had my cock out of my shorts and deep in the wetness of her mouth.

I groaned with pleasure and stared at the scene. Kate had flicked her long, blonde hair to the side and she was sucking up and down on my cock. Her boobs were touching my legs as she sucked me and I worked my hands down to hold them. Her skin was so soft, and yet her boobs were so big and firm. I squeezed them gently and tried to commit the feeling to memory. I never wanted to forget how good she felt.

Then, Kate kissed her way up my body until she was close enough to whisper in my ear. "I want you to fuck me," she breathed. "I want you to fuck me *now*."

"One thing, first," I said, and I rolled her over onto her back. I pulled my shorts off completely so that I was naked, with the sun on my back and the wind reaching all the unusual areas. I knelt over her chest, with my hard dick at the ready. My dick was wet from Kate's mouth and I worked it in between her boobs. She pushed them together for me and I thrusted between them, delighting in how sexy it looked and how masculine it made me feel to dominate this woman. To fuck her unbelievable boobs whilst she lay on her back on the beach and accommodated me. I slapped my dick against her boobs and then moved up to her mouth and she sucked me again, getting my dick wet with her saliva once more.

I'd fucked her mouth and her boobs. Now, I wanted to fuck Kate Upton's pussy.

I pulled her bikini bottoms down and then she spread her legs for me and I moved into their embrace. I rubbed my dick against her clit and briefly considered licking her out, but I couldn't wait any longer and she seemed eager to have my dick inside her. "Fuck me hard," she urged, looking up at me and holding her boobs in her hands.

I was all too happy to oblige.

I slid my cock into her pussy and we shared a moan of pleasure at the sensation. Her pussy was tight and wet and my big shaft went deep inside of her. I fucked her slowly at first, swaying my hips and watching the expression of need on her face as she arched her back and grabbed at my waist, trying to pull me harder into her. Finally, I obliged her and suddenly slammed into her, making her gasp and her boobs bounce. I couldn't get enough of that view as I fucked her and her perfect boobs bounced and she moaned in pleasure. She came to orgasm quickly and I felt her hips bucking against me whilst I continued to slide my hard cock in and out of her wet pussy. "Don't stop," she groaned, clutching at her own boobs. I pulled out from her and rolled her over on the sand. She rose onto her hands and knees and pressed herself back onto my dick. I knelt there in the sand, not moving, letting Kate work her hips against my hard shaft in doggy style. I reached around and felt her boobs and then pulled her upright whilst still on her knees. Now, I could feel my cock sliding hard up against the front wall of her wet pussy and it felt extraordinary. Holding onto her bouncing boobs, I fucked her from behind.

I felt the orgasm building and I wasn't sure if I could finish inside of her. I pulled out and stood up and Kate got the idea. She turned and opened her mouth for me. I guided my dick into her mouth and fucked her for a few more moments and then I pulled away and, amazingly, I came all over her perfect, big, firm, bouncy boobs. I groaned and my knees went weak. Amazing!

I collapsed into the sand and we lay there for a while, panting and moaning. I glanced over at Kate, with my cum all over her tits, laying there in the sand on our own little private beach. This was what dreams were made of. I was living it.

"Round two, big boy?" Kate asked after a while, grinning sexily.

Fuck yes.

Halle Berry

The storm had come in from the Atlantic and it was showing no signs of abating. However, given that I was staying near the top floor of The Plaza hotel in New York City, I wasn't about to take the stairs. The elevator doors opened with a ping and I caught my breath. I knew that the big names often frequented this hotel – that had been part of the allure in the first place. But here, right now, standing in the elevator and looking at me expectantly, presumably having just come down from the Penthouse on the floors above mine, was Halle Berry.

I swallowed. "Hi," I said, nodding to her. She was fucking gorgeous.

Halle just raised her eyebrows and looked as if she was thoroughly amused.

Then, with a ping, the elevator doors started closing again.

"Shit," I realized. I leapt across the threshold and almost bowled right into the movie star in the process. "Sorry," I said, regaining my balance as the elevator began its descent through the bowls of the building. "Almost missed it there."

"Yah huh," Halle agreed. "Nearly missed it."

Then, abruptly, we were tossed to the floor like rag dolls as the elevator came to a screeching halt and the lights flickered and died. We were plunged into darkness for a moment, before a small, red emergency light in the corner came on.

We held our breath and waited for a second.

Nothing happened.

"Oh, you have *got* to be kidding me," Halle cursed, not bothering to get back to her feet. Instead, she turned and sat with her back pressed against the walls.

"What's happening?" I asked.

"Haven't you noticed that storm out there?" Halle asked, pointing up at nowhere in particular. "The power's gone out."

"Damn," I said, unsure of what else to say. Honestly, the building could fall over for all I cared, just so long as I was stuck in this elevator with Halle Berry, I wasn't about to complain.

Doing my best to appear masculine, I got to my feet and tried opening the doors. They didn't budge an inch. I moved around the inside of the elevator, occasionally prodding and touching things and appearing thoughtful, as if I could find a way out.

"There's a hatch up there," Halle commented, pointing.

Sure enough, there was a hatch. "I don't want to jump in here right now," I said, looking up at the hatch. It was just beyond my reach. "The elevator might fall or something."

"Here," Halle extended her hand and I hauled her to her feet. "Give me a boost."

"Ah," I shuffled around a little, trying to figure out how best to lift the movie star. "Here." I crouched down and she swung her legs across my shoulders. I stood up slowly. "Can you reach it?" I asked.

She didn't answer, but I heard her open the hatch. The was air was still in the shaft outside the elevator. No sound could be heard. "It's completely dark out there," Halle said. "I'm not sure if it's a good idea to try to climb out."

"Ok." I sank to my knees and she clambered off my shoulders. "Well I guess we just have to wait then."

The realization seemed to hit Halle that she was stuck indefinitely in an elevator with a total stranger and she turned her eyes on me. For a woman that I presumed was surrounded almost 24/7 by a bodyguard, she didn't appear at all threatened by the situation. In fact, she was very confident. "Is that a British accent I detect?" she asked.

"Ah, pretty close," I said. *Miles off.* "I'm from New Zealand."

"I've heard that it's lovely there," Halle said.

"You've been well informed," I said with a wink.

"You play a strange type of football down there, right?"

"Ah, rugby?" I suggested.

"Yeah," Halle agreed. "Rugby. That must explain those shoulders of yours."

My heart rate tripled. Here we were, trapped in an elevator, and Halle Berry had just told me I had nice shoulders. Her intentions were perfectly clear and I decided then and there that I wasn't about to wait around and risk having the power come back on. I was going to push my chips all in and hope for the best.

"Mmm, you like my shoulders, huh?" I said, smiling and approaching her, trapping her in the corner. She didn't seem to mind. "There's plenty more for you to like."

Halle bumped into the elevator wall, but she was eyeing me up and down with her tongue pressed between her teeth. "Oh, I don't doubt that," she breathed.

With that, I put my hands on the wall on either side of her head and kissed her on the lips. Her lips were excruciatingly soft and my cock was instantly rock hard. Illuminated by the soft emergency lighting, Halle pulled my shirt off over my head and pressed her hands against my chest as my hands crept up her shirt and found her bosom. I fondled her boobs, loving how soft and delicate she felt against me. I had her shirt off in a hurry and her bra shortly followed.

Wow.

Topless and illuminated by the soft red glow of the emergency light, Halle Berry looked positively delicious. I hungered for her and I tugged at her jeans. She kicked her shoes off and stepped out of her jeans so that she was standing before me in just her knickers. I pressed her up against the walls of the elevator and she wrapped her legs around my waist, moaning and thrusting herself against me, seemingly as eager as I was.

Halle unzipped my trousers and tugged them down my legs. I shoved my underwear down after them so that I was standing naked now. I pressed her head down towards my chest, eager to feel her mouth around my dick, but she resisted the pull.

I shrugged inwardly. *So, she doesn't suck dick apparently.* I was disappointed, but I wasn't about to let that spoil the moment. I hoisted her further up the wall instead and put my arms underneath her legs. I kissed the inside of her thighs and rubbed my chin against her pussy. I could feel the wetness seeping through her knickers. I pulled the material aside and licked her pussy. Halle cried out and her hands grabbed at the wall, grasping for something to hold onto as I licked her out. Her hips thrust against me, desperate for more. The woman was crazy!

I licked her out for a few minutes; building up the tension and listening to her cries of pleasure as they reached a crescendo.

"*Fuck,*" she gasped as I pulled away and lowered her to the ground. "Don't stop. I'm so close!"

"My turn," I said, ripping her knickers off and grabbing her by the hips. I spun her around so that she was facing the wall again and I bent her over in front of me.

"Oh, FUUUUCCCKKK!" Halle screamed as I slid my throbbing hard dick into her dripping wet pussy. "*Fuck*!"

"Fuck yeah," I groaned back at her, grabbing her by her hips and thrusting desperately against her. I felt crazed with lust for this woman. She was unbelievably wet. I had never experienced a woman quite so wet before and it felt amazing in the extreme. I slapped her arse and pounded her even harder still, pulling her against me, making sure every last inch of my rock hard cock got inside that incredible, movie-star pussy. I reached around and held her boobs with one hand whilst I tugged at her black hair with the other. Her boobs were bouncing and they felt so unbelievably good.

I was fucking Halle Berry.

I was bending her over in an elevator, pulling her hair, slapping her arse, feeling her boobs and making her scream with pleasure as I fucked her.

The tension was building and I grabbed Halle and lifted her onto me as I lay down on the ground. Now, she was riding me reverse-cowgirl style and she was fucking extraordinary at it. She bounced on my dick and screamed with wild abandon as she slammed herself desperately down onto me; impaling herself on my large dick.

Suddenly, the lights came back on in the elevator and Halle gasped.

"Oh, *fuck no!*" I growled.

Please tell me this isn't happening! Not now!

"Keep going," I urged. "I'm going to come inside you."

Halle didn't need to be told twice. She quickly stood and turned around so that she was facing me and then lowered herself onto my dick once again. Now I could see her face as she screamed in pleasure and her big boobs as she bounced on top of me.

We still had a long way down to go and the elevator seemed to be pretty slow, given that it was an old building. The mounting tension all added to the experience and, before I knew it, I was clutching Halle against me and bucking and groaning as I came inside her tight little pussy. Halle was moaning just as fervently as she too reached a climax and shared the moment of pleasure with me.

My dick throbbed inside the movie star but we both knew that the moment couldn't last much longer.

"Fuck," Halle groaned and then pushed herself off of me. Hot cum dripped from her pussy as she leapt into her clothes. I followed suit and we got ourselves in order just as the elevator came to a halt and the doors opened.

"Well, it was a pleasure meeting you," Halle said, winking at me as she exited the elevator doors. "Perhaps I'll have to visit New Zealand someday."

A pleasure indeed.

Jessica Alba

"You're going to crash us into those rocks, Rick!" she exclaimed, pointing.

"I got it, I got it," Rick said as reassuringly as possible, spinning the wheel and peering ahead at the waves as they reared up toward the bow of the yacht. *Perhaps taking her sailing hadn't been the best idea?* he pondered. The sun was out and it would've been a beautiful day indeed were it not for the relentless pounding of the swell.

Rick had been dating Jessica Alba for just over a month now and he had wanted to surprise her and do something special and memorable together. He had convinced his brother to lend him his yacht and give a crash course in sailing. In his head, Rick had envisioned smooth waters, lazily swinging hammocks, flapping sails, fishing rods buzzing and the unbelievable, naked body of his famous girlfriend as she tanned on the deck and then passionate, mind blowing sex – the kind that the couple had become accustomed to. Rick recalled their first night together when he had cooked dinner for Jessica and then they had sipped at wine on the couch and played scrabble. Scrabble had turned into a kiss and then the kiss turned into hands feeling along bare thighs and under clothes and then, before he knew it, Rick had found himself reclining on the sofa with Jessica Alba perfectly naked and riding his dick, moaning and flashing that sexy smile at him as she worked her pussy up and down his thick shaft. Now, staring glumly out at the gathering waves, Rick couldn't help but think that he may have bitten off more than he could chew with this particular venture; not that he was about to let on any of his misgivings to Jessica. Externally, he was the iceman – as calm and unflappable as could be. On the inside however, Rick was rehearsing the procedure for grabbing a lifebuoy and jumping overboard and perhaps starting a new life in turtle conservation.

"Why don't we go in there?" Jessica suggested, pointing again.

Rick followed her hand and saw that she was pointing into a little bay that appeared to be protected from the swell. It was a great idea. "Great idea," Rick called back to her over the thunderous crashing of the ocean. He spun the wheel fiercely in the other direction and they were both jerked in their seats as the sails suddenly filled with wind and shot them towards the protection of the bay, like a racehorse out of the gates.

The effect of the harbor was astonishing, like stepping inside from a storm. Here, the swell died away to nothing and there was not a breath of wind to be felt. The sun shone heavily and the temperature seemed to climb by 10 degrees. "Good call," Rick said gratefully, steering the boat gently in further behind the headland and then releasing the anchor. "What do you say we just hang out in here for a few hours? We'll wait for this swell to die down and then cruise on back to the dock."

Jessica smiled. Such a cute smile. Adorable and sexy. "Sure thing," she said. "It's lovely here! And we have it all to ourselves, too!"

Rick glanced around. Sure enough, there were no other boats and there was no beach or houses. The water simply lapped up against the mangroves and rocks. By a sheer stroke of luck, they had found the place that Rick had been daydreaming about. It was perfect.

Rick walked out onto the deck and spread his arms to enjoy the feeling of the sun on his skin. It was such a relief to have ceased the incessant tossing and turning of the swell. Suddenly, Rick felt hands around his waist and Jessica's lips at his ears. "Want to fuck me here?" she whispered, brushing her hand tantalizingly across his manhood. It stood to attention immediately.

"What do *you* think?" Rick breathed incredulously, following the movements of her hands on his body.

Jessica breathed and moaned in his ear sexily for him and ran her hands up his chest before yanking his shirt up over his head. The sun felt glorious but it was Jessica Alba that had all of Rick's attention. "Sit," she demanded with a little giggle and she pushed him towards a part of the hull that presented itself as a natural, unmoving chair.

Rick sat and gazed up at Jessica as she pulled her shirt off over her head to reveal that she wasn't wearing a bra underneath. Her perfect little breasts shone in the sunlight and she tossed her shirt onto the deck, with eyes only for her man.

Rick couldn't stop his feet from tapping impatiently.

Jessica walked towards him, her hips swaying tantalizingly as she pushed her skirt down off her hips until she was completely naked and within arm's reach of him.

Rick groaned lustfully. His dick was throbbing and hard, yearning to be inside this woman. She was so perfectly lithe and supple and athletic and her smile could light up the night.

With a soundtrack of waves lapping gently against the hull of the yacht, Jessica threw her leg over Rick and straddled his lap, with her boobs in his face and her hands in his hair. She pressed herself against the hardness of his cock and she leant in to whisper in his ear. "I want to suck your dick," she breathed and she ran her tongue delicately along his neck whilst she gyrated and grinded her hips against him, with nothing but a thin layer of fabric to restrain his dick from entering her soft, wet pussy. "I want you to slap it against my face and my tits and I want to lick it and kiss it," she breathed, moaning softly as she rubbed her clit against him. "I want to put it down my throat and suck on it until you're about to explode," she said.

Rick felt as if he was about to explode already.

"But most of all," Jessica whispered, and she pressed Rick's lips to her boobs. "I want to feel your dick inside my pussy. Deep inside me."

"Well then, what are we waiting for?" Rick groaned, and he picked Jessica up, with her legs wrapped around his waist, and he lay her down on the deck of the yacht, completely naked and splayed out before him. Her legs were spread, inviting him in. Rick didn't wait around and he made straight for that sweetness between her legs. She was wet and sweet and she squealed softly and her hips bucked as Rick worked his tongue around her clit. He pulled away briefly and pulled his clothes off as quickly as possible so that he was naked as well. Jessica lay back and teased him in with a single finger, inviting his cock closer. Rick knelt beside her and pushed his dick into her mouth whilst he held the back of her head. She looked at him with those delicate eyes whilst he fucked her mouth and he felt as if he could come already, but he didn't want to. Not yet.

Normally, Rick would've let her suck his dick for ten minutes or more, she was so good at it, but today he was feeling impatient. He pressed himself down between Jessica's long, soft legs and felt her wrap her legs around his waist as he rubbed his rock solid dick against her clit, teasing her with anticipation.

"Give it to me!" Jess almost squealed, grabbing Rick by the hips and pulling him closer.

Relenting, Rick pushed his dick into that tight, wet seam and they both groaned in unison as he fell deeply into her pussy. Wet and glorious.

They stayed that way for some time before Rick starting moving; long and slow thrusts into Jessica Alba's pussy, listening to her moan in time with each movement. She tightened her pussy muscles around his shaft and it felt extraordinary.

Rick increased his speed. Harder and faster. Jess's boobs started bouncing as he slammed into her and she moaned and threw her head back in wild abandon. She belonged to him. He could do whatever he wanted to her. Rick fucked her hard, feeling her legs around him and watching her tits bounce and relishing the look of pure delight on her face as she reached a body-jerking orgasm underneath him.

Rick let her finish and relax a little bit before standing her up and turning her around. He bent her forwards over the small railing fence that ran around the perimeter of the deck and he took a moment to enjoy the view of her ass, presented for him perfectly. Her soft, supple and smooth legs reaching on seemingly forever. Her pussy was dripping – waiting for him.

Rick guided his dick into her from behind and groaned as he sunk even deeper into her. Jess responded by throwing her head back and Rick caught her hair and held it whilst he fucked her tight little body. He relinquished his grip on her hair for a tighter grip on her hips and he smacked her ass and she squealed for him.

The tension built and Rick groaned and bucked his hips, slamming his dick as deeply into that perfect pussy as he could as he finished and sent his hot cum deep inside Jessica Alba.

Heaven truly is a place on Earth.

Jennifer Aniston

 I moved through the press of bodies as they pulsed and gyrated against each other. Everybody was still warming up and getting themselves comfortable. I saw a few couples fucking discreetly in the corners of the rooms, but for the most part, men and women were dancing or lounging about and watching the performers on the stages.

 Everyone was wearing masks, myself included. It felt surreal. This was my first time attending an anonymous sex party and I was excited about what I might experience. Already, I was seeing things that I had never seen before. I had never watched others having sex – not in real life, only on porn websites – now I was seeing it for real. Ultra high-definition. As real as it gets.

 Girls could be heard moaning over the top of the seductive music as their male partners fucked them in the dark corners of the rooms. There were hidden partitions and curtains and sofas everywhere, with each new turn unveiling a new room of sex and intrigue. There was a soft, red glow that appeared to be suffusing everything and it was turning everybody's skin the colour of warm gold. There was a strict dress code. Underwear was permitted to be worn, but absolutely nothing else. Most people that I saw were already naked. Some girls were wearing lingerie and swaying their hips in time with the music. It was still early days and everyone was looking for partners.

 I stood with my back against the wall for a while and watched the performers on the stage nearest me. There were two girls dancing naked on a pole and kissing and touching each other. As I watched, a naked guy with a massive erection climbed up onto the stage and the girls knelt in front of him and started sucking his dick. The masks covered the top half of everyone's faces, leaving just small holes for the eyes. It was a strange effect. Apparently it was based on something that the Ancient Romans used to do when they held orgies in their villas where the aristocrats could fuck the hosts' slave girls and guys.

As I watched, one of the girls on the stage stood up and turned around, bending over slightly and pressing her chest against the pole so that her tits wrapped around it on either side. The guy eagerly came up from behind and entered her, standing doggy-style. The girl moaned and called out over the top of the music as the guy held her hips and fucked her urgently. The other girl slipped off the stage and straddled another man's lap, who was sitting on one of the sofas and watching the performance. She pressed his face into her massive boobs and rubbed her naked clit against him.

I was only wearing underwear and my erection was plain to see. The environment was incredibly sexy and my body was eager to get involved.

A woman approached me. Through the holes in her mask, I saw her eyes looking me up and down and lingering on the bulge in my underwear. She was topless, but she was wearing a lacy g-string and high heels. She walked right up to me until her waist was pressing lightly against my erect penis and she smiled seductively. Then, she turned and stepped away from me. She pressed her hands against the back of a sofa and bent over, smiling over her shoulder at me as she presented her ass for me to look at.

I returned the smile.

The woman was absolutely stunning. Perfect figure.

Without another word, the woman reached down to her own hips and slipped the g-string down to her ankles, swaying her hips as she went and then stepping out of the fabric. Aside from the high heels, she was now completely naked and I was utterly entranced.

She turned back to me and approached again. I was still leaning against the wall, with my hard dick bulging for all the world to see. The lady stepped right up to me again and we kissed on the lips. Then she kissed neck and moaned in my ear and I felt her hands gliding down my hips and gently caressing my manhood. I started with my hands touching her naked hips. I reached up and cupped her boobs as we kissed, delighting in the shape and supple skin of her breasts. Then, when I couldn't stand it anymore, I grabbed her ass and pulled her against me and we kissed in earnest. She wrapped her legs around my waist. "Take me to a room," she moaned in my ear. "I want you to fuck me."

I carried her through a thin curtain and laid her down on a silky mattress that was waiting. There was another couple fucking on a sofa nearby. The woman was riding her man's cock and moaning as her tits bounced. I could hardly wait to feel my own woman riding me, with her wet pussy sliding up and down my dick.

I stood and slipped my underwear off. I was naked in a club full of strangers and I was loving the experience. I briefly wondered if I should wear a condom, but my partner didn't seem to think so. She knelt in front of me and, smiling up at me, she wrapped her mouth around my cock and started sucking it. I groaned and turned to watch the couple fucking on the sofa again. Those bouncing tits were hypnotic and the girl was moaning delightfully.

I enjoyed the blowjob for a few minutes and then licked out my lady, returning the favour. I had never really enjoyed giving oral before, but this woman tasted wonderful and her bucking hips and small squeals of pleasure turned me on even more.

Staying between her legs, I kissed my way up her body until I felt my dick lightly touching her soaking wet pussy. I kissed her neck and lowered my hips as slowly as I could.

The lady gasped and she scratched my back as I pushed my dick into her luxurious wetness. I fucked her slowly for a while, moving in time with the slow rhythm of the music that was pulsing throughout the club. I watched her tits bounce slowly and listened to her gasping as I thrusted between her long, smooth legs.

I had never fucked a complete stranger before and I was loving the experience. I didn't even know the woman's name, but I knew what her pussy felt like, I knew that she gave amazing blowjobs and I knew that she had gorgeous tits and an amazing body. The girl could've been a movie star.

As I fucked her on her back, another woman approached and watched us for a few moments before climbing onto the mattress and resting her knees on either side of my woman's face, with her back to me. She knelt there and my woman licked her pussy whilst I fucked her. A regular threesome. *This was fucking awesome!*

The girl on top then backed up and bent over in front of me and started kissing my partner with her pussy presented for me. I pulled out of my girl and grinned as I heard her groan with disappointment. I grabbed the new girl by her hips and entered her from behind, thrusting harder and faster now. I slapped her ass and pounded her, making her tits bounce in front of my woman underneath.

The girl screamed out loud as I fucked her and I felt gazes turning to watch us from around the room. I decided I wanted to fuck my original woman again and I pulled away from the doggy-style girl. She squealed with disappointment as I pulled away and collapsed sideways onto the mattress. As she did so, something must've caught my partner's mask, because it slipped sideways off her face for the briefest of moments.

I gasped in shock.

I recognized her!

She quickly rearranged the mask and I knew that nobody else had seen her face, but I knew who she was. I smiled at her to let her know her secret was safe and she returned the smile and rolled over onto her hands and knees.

I pulled her hips back towards me and entered her again in the same manner as I had fucked the other girl.

I was fucking Jennifer Aniston!

She really was a movie star.

The other girl rolled onto her back and began fingering herself whilst I fucked Jen.

After a time, Jen grabbed my arm and pulled me down onto the mattress with the two girls so that I was lying on my back. The other girl stopped fingering herself and got to her knees, but Jen was having none of it. She quickly straddled my lap and used her hands to guide my dick into her pussy as she lowered herself onto me. I stared at her as she started riding my cock, bouncing up and down and grabbing her own boobs and moaning as she fucked me. The other girl approached and started kissing my neck. I felt up her boobs and her legs and her ass as she kissed me and whilst Jen continued to bounce her tight, wet pussy down on my dick. It was utterly luxurious.

From my vantage point on the bed, I glanced around the room.

There were threesomes and couples and foursomes fucking and giving oral everywhere the eye could see. There were girls screaming and moaning and boobs bouncing and asses being slapped as hips bucked and pounded against each other.

I saw a guy pull away from two girls that were on their knees in front of him and had been sucking his dick, and he beat himself off and came on their faces and their tits.

As I watched, Jen rose up off my dick and pulled the other girls head down towards my dick and I felt the warmth of her mouth as she started sucking me. Jen looked sweaty and she smiled and winked at me through her mask as the other girl sucked me off.

I smiled back.

I was ready to come and I knew who I wanted to come inside.

I pulled the girl back up to my neck and Jennifer Aniston lowered herself back onto my dick with a pleasurable moan and she resumed her riding.

I was feeling up my other girls' tits as the pressure built, before, finally, I bucked and groaned and Jen slammed her pussy hard onto me, forcing my dick deep inside of her as I reached orgasm and squirted my hot cum inside of her. Jen gasped and threw her head back as she felt the hot cum in her pussy and she swayed her hips against me some more, eliciting every possible ounce of pleasure from the experience.

All around us, guys were groaning as they came on faces and boobs and inside wet pussy's and mouths as the orgy reached a mutual climax point and the music throbbed within the walls.

That was the most incredible sexual experience of my life. I would be coming back here for damned sure; I just hoped that Jen would be returning also.

She was sweaty and slumped against my chest, but she winked and smiled at me and giggled a little bit, like she felt shy now that it was over.

I knew what that wink meant.

She would be returning also.

Kim Kardashian

The music was throbbing. Andrew could feel it inside of his chest as he walked down the stairs. The place was alive and the energy hung in the air like a mist. Or maybe it was smoke? Andrew didn't really care. He was drunk and now he wanted to find a girl to take home with him.

He made a beeline for the dance floor.

There was a crush of bodies in front of the DJ. The place was completely packed. Apparently there was some VIP party thing going on at the club, but Andrew didn't really care about any of that. Celebrities didn't faze him one way or the other.

He got to dancing and soon had a sexy little teeny bopper grinding her mini-skirt clad ass up against him. Andrew was used to the attention. He often felt that he could fuck whoever he wanted. He was a man in demand. He felt that the dancing girl was possibly too young for him, so he wasn't going to take her home, but she was sexy, so he felt up her hips and her ass as she danced and gave her a quick kiss before moving on.

Soon, Andrew was near the middle of the crush of people and he let himself dance and enjoy the drunken haze. He saw guys in suits standing amongst the dancing crowd. They looked eerie, standing completely still whilst everybody else was perpetually moving. The guys in suits were glaring at anybody and everybody. Andrew held their gaze and glared right back. He was a regular at the club and all of the staff there knew him. He could do whatever the fuck he wanted. He figured the guys must have been bodyguards for the celebrities that were allegedly mingling amongst the throng of bodies.

Andrew felt hands near his waist and he ignored it for a moment. The crush of bodies made the groping action invisible to anybody looking. The hands became more insistent and they soon moved towards his dick and started squeezing gently.

Wanting to make sure it was a girl touching him and not Elton John, Andrew turned around and found himself face to face with a woman that he vaguely recognized. The face was smiling suggestively at him.

Kim Kardashian, a small voice in his head said informingly.

Andrew shrugged. He didn't care what her name was. The woman was sexy, she had her tits on display in a tight black dress and she had her hands on his dick when he was drunk and horny.

She would do.

Andrew returned the smile and put his hands on Kim's hips and spun her around so that he was pressed up against her, front-to-back. He felt her ass grinding deliberately and suggestively against his cock as they danced together.

Andrew felt himself getting hard, and he pressed himself tighter against the Kardashian girl so that she could feel it too. She acknowledged the erection with a groping hand and a light squeeze. Her hips appeared to be in perpetual motion down there and Andrew was enjoying the display of flirting.

One of the bodyguards in the black suits began to approach through the crowd. Perhaps he didn't like Andrew's dance moves. Perhaps he was interested in a dance-off.

Andrew didn't care, but Kim did. She turned around and pulled Andrew's head down so that she could be heard over the deafening thud of the music. "Here comes a buzz-kill," she said.

I just nodded and shrugged.

Oh well.

There were plenty of other girls in the club, all just as sexy and just as slutty as the Kardashian girl, and most of them weren't accompanied by bodyguards. But Kim wasn't prepared to give up just yet.

"Wait," she said, and she grabbed Andrew's hand and forced it down between her thighs where nobody could see.

Andrew let his hand get dragged up the inside of her thigh and soon discovered that Kim wasn't wearing any underwear beneath her party dress. Of even more interest to Andrew however, was the fact that she was already dripping wet.

The chick was about to have an orgasm right there on the dance floor.

Too easy.

Andrew nodded and grabbed her wrist in return. "Come on, then," he said, and he steered her away from the approaching bodyguard. Andrew trusted in the crush of the crowd to hide their escape and slow the approach of anymore guards. The whole thing was very exciting. The music continued to pound away and revelers danced on relentlessly, oblivious to the game of celebrity cat and mouse that was unfolding in their midst.

Andrew led Kim towards a roped off area. There were stairs beyond the rope, leading upwards and downwards. Upstairs was the accommodation area. Andrew knew that because he had stayed there for a few years previously. Downstairs was the emergency exit.

There was a bouncer at the rope. He glanced at Andrew, looked at Kim and then laughed and unclipped the rope for them. Andrew dragged Kim through and led her down the stairs.

There were staff toilets down there, but Andrew knew that nobody ever used them. They were dank and unkempt. He pushed through the door and Kim followed, hot on his heels. She didn't seem too fussed by the dirty surroundings. Perhaps this wasn't her first time in a toilet stall.

Even down there, the music was throbbing throughout the room, although it was muffled slightly.

"Come on, then," Andrew said again, grabbing Kim by her waist and pushing her up against a wall. He was a man in demand and he had no time for messing about. He got straight into it. He kissed and bit the Kardashian woman on her neck and pressed himself up against her, forcing her back against the wall. She groaned and ran her hands through his hair.

Andrew felt his way around her hips and then grabbed her voluptuous ass and squeezed it and pulled her harder against him, grinding his hard dick against her pelvic bone.

Nice ass, Andrew thought as he felt her up. *Perhaps I'll fuck her from behind to get a good look at it.*

First things first, though.

Andrew grabbed Kim behind her neck and pulled her head downwards. He unbuckled his jeans with his other hand and felt the air around his privates as he got his dick out and presented it. Half a second later, Andrew groaned and arched his head back to stare at the ceiling as he felt the wet lips and tongue wrap around the shaft of his aching hard cock.

It was dark in the toilets. They were illuminated only by a small, flickering neon light at the far end of the room.

Even if someone came in, they might not have noticed the blowjob action that was going on, because they were mostly hidden in the shadows.

After a few minutes, Andrew got impatient. Kim's mouth felt as good as any other woman's and she wasn't blowing his mind with her blowjob skills. He grabbed her by the arm and stood her back up again, thinking about her ass and how good it had felt. He spun her around and pressed her chest up against the wall and lifted her dress so that it was folded up just below her tits, exposing her naked legs, ass and stomach region.

Andrew checked out the view for a few moments and nodded his approval. She had a fine ass, indeed, and a tiny waist. A real hourglass figure, which he liked a lot. To complete the picture, Andrew reached around and pulled the front of her tight black dress aside, exposing her tits. They fit nicely in his hands.

"Fuck me," Kim groaned.

"Shut up," Andrew growled, and he pushed her tits back up against the wall and forced her ass out towards him.

Using his spare hand, he guided his dick into her pussy. He didn't bother starting slow and soft. The woman was soaking wet and craving a good fucking. Andrew pushed the length of his big dick right into her and she screamed, loud enough to be heard clearly over the music. She had fucking loved that.

Andrew grabbed her by her hips and fucked her hard and fast and urgently, watching her ass bounce and wobble as he thrust himself against it. There was no denying the quality of that ass. The music was loud and Kim screamed without restraint.

Andrew slapped that ass as he fucked her and she screamed some more. She came within moments and Andrew felt her hips bucking as she groaned and squealed and arched her back.

Andrew felt his dick slide out of her mouth and he used his own hand to finish the cumshot onto her tits and all over her black dress.

She was going to have some explaining to do.

Andrew stood there panting for a while and then he pulled his jeans up and buckled himself up again. He tipped his imaginary hat to Kim, still kneeling on the floor up against the wall and covered in his cum. He pushed back through the door and climbed back up the stairs, watching the dancing girls as their legs flashed and the tight dresses hugged their bodies.

He still hadn't found a girl to take home with him yet.

Sofia Vergara

I sat for a moment and listened to the soft trickling of water from the ornamental ponds and fountains that adorned the room. I worked long days, but it was very hard to complain about my workspace. As a masseuse, I worked from a small room on the Maldives Island chain, with timber shutters that opened up onto a spectacular view of the Pacific Ocean in the tropics. I had a receptionist in the adjoining room, beautiful, warm weather and sunny days, soft music and water fountains. On my time off, I worked out at the resort gym, drank at the bar, danced on the sand and swam in the crystal clear waters of the lagoon. I lived a life of luxury. My only complaint was my clients. For the most part, they were exquisitely rich, often famous and always rude.

There was a knock on the door and my receptionist poked her head in. "Your 1 o'clock is ready, Jonathan," she said.

"Sofia?" I asked, thinking of the actress from the hit TV show, *Modern Family,* and wondering what she would be like when the cameras were off.

"Yes, Mrs. Vergara," the receptionist confirmed. "Shall I send her in?"

I nodded and stood up again with a weary sigh. "Send her in," I said. It was all part of our routine. *What else was I going to say?*

Sofia Vergara entered the room like a cool breeze on a hot day - refreshing and revitalising. She was wearing a light, see-through skirt and a bright blue bikini top. I could see the matching blue through the thin skirt. Sofia looked at me with warmth in her eyes and she smiled - a first for me when dealing with the rich and famous. Most refreshing indeed.

"Please," I said, gesturing to the waiting table. "Make yourself comfortable. I'll give you a few moments. Call out if you need anything." I stepped out to the ante room and stretched my fingers and gazed out over the guest pool. I could see Sofia's husband there, drinking beer and flirting with one of the resort waitresses. It was nothing unusual. The rules of social etiquette do not apply to the rich and famous.

"I am ready," Sofia called through the thin partition.

I couldn't help but smile at her Columbian accent. I had always suspected that it had been faked on her TV show, but apparently not. It was a delightful accent. Her voice was full of a friendly warmth.

I re-entered the room, just as I had done thousands of times before.

Sofia was lying naked on her stomach on the massage table, with a small white towel covering her ass. She was resting her chin on her forearms and flashing that tantalising smile at me. "I feel like I have been sitting on airplanes for weeks!" she exclaimed, groaning and stretching her back slightly to emphasise her point. "I have been told that you have the magic touch."

I smiled politely, enjoying her company and ease of conversation. "Well, let me see what I can do about that," I said.

Always the professional.

I began working on her neck, her shoulders and her back. She had smiled at me and been friendly, so I was determined to give her the best possible massage that I could. Being friendly has it's benefits. "Have you been enjoying your stay in the Maldives?" I asked politely as I worked.

Sofia sighed, with her face down. "Oh, yes," she said. "It's lovely here." She paused for a moment, as if considering her next words. Evidently she decided to threw caution to the wind, because she continued. "I wish my husband would stop fucking the staff," she said. "But aside from that, it is beautiful here."

My eyes widened at her candid talk. "Oh," I said, unsure what the correct response should be. "I'm saddened to hear that," I decided to say. And then I pressed on recklessly, because she had smiled at me. "A beautiful woman such as yourself - I think you deserve much better treatment than that."

Sofia didn't respond for a moment.

And then she moved.

I gasped in shock as she propped herself up onto her elbows - her bare breasts on display - and asked, "do you really think I am beautiful?" She was smiling at me as she said it. Smiling in a vulnerable way. Her exposed boobs were breathtaking in their perfection.

"The most beautiful client I've ever had," I said, and honestly. "And I've had a lot of beautiful clients."

Sofia smiled again. "Do you think you could treat me better?" she asked. Her voice dripped with sexuality and suggestion. I almost melted into the floor.

"I could treat you however you wanted to be treated," I managed to say, doing my best to return the sexuality in my voice.

"That's what I want to hear," Sofia said. That delightful accent. She reached out with her hand and grabbed the waistband of my trousers. "If my husband can fuck the staff, then so can I," Sofia said. She pulled me closer toward her. Before I even had time to think, Sofia had pulled the front of trousers down and my hard dick was in her mouth.

I stood at the head of my own massage table as Sofia Vergara sucked on my dick and moaned to let me know that she was enjoying it. Her mouth felt phenomenal. Warm and wet. I could feel her throat vibrating as she moaned.

She propped herself up further on her elbows and I massaged her big boobs. They felt full and firm. Perfection.

I felt an orgasm building and I was about to cum inside Sofia's mouth when I remembered my promise to treat her well. I pulled away and felt the orgasm recede. That had been close. "Your turn, beautiful," I said.

I walked around the bench and Sofia rolled herself over for me, flicking the small towel out of the way. I spread her legs with my hands and kissed along the length of her legs. She moaned softly as I drew closer and closer to her pussy. Finally, I licked her out and her hips bucked and jerked and I felt her hands gripping my hair as I worked my tongue around her juicy clit.

I clambered up onto the bench on top of her and I was astonished at how good she looked on her back. She was smiling up at me, with her perfect tits out on display and her toned abs working as she arched her back to present herself for me. I pushed my dick into her wet pussy very slowly. The head of my dick entered her and then the entire length of my shaft and Sofia's expression of pleasure on her face made me think that perhaps I was in heaven and I had my hard dick inside the heavenly pussy of an angel.

I fucked her hard and fast right from the outset. We didn't have all night together. She had a 45 minute massage appointment and her husband was only 50 meters away, lounging by the pool and flirting with waitresses whilst I fucked his gorgeous wife.

Celebrity pussy, I thought to myself.

Sofia couldn't help herself and she cried out and then clamped a hand to her mouth again.

I briefly wondered if anyone else had heard it and then forgot all about it, because I was staring at Sofia Vergara's perfect ass as I fucked her on her hands and knees on my massage table.

The tension built until, finally, just as our 45 minutes elapsed, I reached an orgasm and finished inside Sofia, with my hands hard on her hips, forcing my dick and cum as deeply into her as I could - which was very deep.

Sofia gasped and arched her head up as she felt the hot cum inside of her and I grabbed her hair and pulled her back towards me. I kissed and bit her neck as I finished inside of her and felt her tits with my spare hand. I was determined to remember this fuck for the rest of my life.

I could no longer complain about my celebrity clients. They were fucking extraordinary.

Megan Fox

"Now, pout for me," Angelo said, glancing over the top of his camera at his subject to confirm that she was obeying him.

She was.

Megan Fox pouted her lips for the camera and slightly squinted her eyes and pushed her jaw out subtly, just as she had been taught.

"Good girl," Angelo cooed, returning to his viewfinder and clicking away like mad. He captured Megan's sex appeal from every angle before asking her for another outfit and another pose. Angelo loved his job. He got to work with the hottest celebrities in Hollywood - telling them what to wear and how to pose whilst he photographed them in his studio and then got paid for the privilege.

"Now the white one, thanks honey," Angelo instructed, pointing to the white lingerie that was next on the clothes rack.

Angelo pulled up the photos on his computer whilst Megan changed out of her bright red bikini and stepped into the lacy underwear in front of him. Angelo offered a small curtain behind which his celebrities could change if they wished, but most of them were neither shy nor modest when it came to getting naked in his studio. The celebrities that he dealt with were at their very best when they visited Angelo. Invariably, they all loved photo shoots, because it was all about them and their ego, and Angelo was an expert in making the celebrities feel sexy. That confidence needed to come across in the photos. Angelo was a constant stream of flattery, and so the female celebs often undressed in front of him, simply to elicit more compliments.

"God, that ass belongs on a billboard, honey," Angelo commented, glancing away from his computer to check out Megan Fox's naked ass as she pulled down her red bikini bottoms.

Megan smiled over her shoulder at him and Angelo winked and returned to his computer screen. The photos were coming out well, but they weren't much different to the last shoots that he had done with Megan. He felt that his publishers would be looking for more variety this time from one of the hottest celebrities in the modern world.

Turning back to check out Megan's ass as she bent over again, Angelo had a lightbulb moment. He knew what the publishers wanted. It was his job to provide. Megan might not like it, but then again, she just might.

"Have you met Jorge before, Miss Fox?" Angelo asked, standing up from his computer and approaching Megan. He made subtle adjustments to her bra, pushing her boobs around to make them sit up for the camera.

"Is he the one with the muscles?" Megan asked.

"That's the one," Angelo said, nodding. He knew fully well that all of his celebrities were aware of Jorge and the services that he provided. "Would you like to meet him today?" Angelo asked casually. He finished adjusting her outfit and smacked her ass to give it his tick of approval.

Megan giggled slightly and bit her finger, as if she was giving the proposition serious thought. "Me and Jorge?" she said. "Today?"

"You will have the best time, honey," Angelo said. "You will just love it, I promise. Jorge can be very gentle."

"Oh, I hope not!" Megan exclaimed.

That's a yes, Angelo knew. " I'll send for him," he said, smiling warmly and pulling out his phone. "You make yourself comfortable, sexy girl. You're getting that sweet little ass fucked today."

Angelo arranged for a four poster bed to be wheeled into the studio and checked his lighting situation. He was happy with everything.

Megan lay herself on the bed, looking much like a gift, just waiting to be unwrapped.

Jorge arrived shortly after. He was wearing a mask across his eyes and nothing else.

Immediately, Megan noticed the size of his swinging dick and she gasped and turned to look at Angelo with a twinkle in her eyes.

Jorge was huge. Eleven inches of thick meat.

Angelo set some of the cameras to record video and then he prepared himself to hover around the edges, taking still shots with his favourite lense.

Jorge didn't wait for an invitation or an introduction. He had done this many times before.

Angelo watched and started clicking away immediately as Jorge kissed Megan and then ripped off her small white bra and knickers. His hands went straight to her boobs and her ass and Megan's hands went straight for the big hunk of meat between Jorge's legs. She caressed his dick and then gasped as Jorge grabbed her by the back of her head and pulled her head down towards his dick.

Megan hesitated slightly as she appraised the large penis from close-up, and then she used both hands to guide it into her mouth.

Angelo smiled to himself as he snapped the photo of Megan Fox with a huge dick in her mouth. He could name his price for a photo like that. Teenage boys could beat off to it in front of their computer screens. Megan's management could say it was a fake and the media would turn all of it's attention towards Megan Fox for 12 months or so and she would score a few big-name movie roles and everybody would win. This was Hollywood after all, and nothing sells better than sex.

The blowjob continued for a few minutes.

Angelo flitted about, snapping the action from different angles. His favourite was the view from behind, where he could capture Megan's naked pussy in a perfect doggy-style position, and still see the cock in her mouth as she glanced over her shoulder.

Perfection.

"Now ride his cock, honey," Angelo called softly. "Get up there, cowgirl."

Jorge lay down in the mattress and Megan straddled his lap carefully, facing the camera, reverse cowgirl style. She handled Jorge's dick - wet from her blowjob - and held it upright whilst she gently lowered herself onto it.

"Oh my god," Megan gasped as the head of his gigantic cock slid inside her pussy.

Angelo caught the open-mouthed gasp perfectly. That moment would be forever preserved in time. Megan Fox lowering herself onto a huge cock.

Megan called out as the cock plunged deeper inside her. She rubbed her clit for a moment as she got used to the thick meat inside her, and then she started riding the dick like a pornstar.

Angelo watched her tits bounce up and down and listened to Megan shouting out as she rode the dick - all the while, he clicked away on his camera, capturing the sex for the rest of the world to enjoy. He could hear a sloppy wet sound as Megan's pussy moved up and down Jorge's shaft. The girl was really enjoying herself up there.

Angelo captured his shots and then nodded to Jorge.

Jorge grabbed Megan by the waist and picked her up, turning her around so that she was kneeling on the bed in the doggy-style position. His dick never left her pussy as he performed the manoeuvre and Megan groaned as she felt the cock reach new places in her pussy.

Jorge slapped her ass and held her hips firmly as he pumped the mega-star with his big cock. His pelvis made a slapping sound as he pounded against her hot ass.

Angelo loved this angle.

He came in close from in front of Megan, just slightly below her eye line, and captured shot after shot of her with her head thrown back, eyes closed, tits at full swing, mouth open in a scream of ecstasy, and with the masked Jorge towering behind her with his hands on her hips.

Glorious.

"Fuck yeah, girl," Angelo exclaimed, wanting to further boost Megan's confidence to see if she might try something bold and daring.

She did exactly that.

Megan opened her eyes and smiled at Angelo as if just noticing him for the first time.

Angelo took a photo of her looking directly into the lense.

Then, Megan reached forward and grabbed Angelo by the waist and dragged him closer to her. Clearly, she had noticed the bulge in Angelo's trousers, because she went straight for his zip and had his erect dick in her hands a moment later. He wasn't as big as Jorge, but Angelo was still generously proportioned.

Jorge laughed as he saw what was happening and he continued to fuck the celebrity slut from behind, slapping her ass eagerly as Megan tried to steer

Angelo's dick into her mouth as she bounced on the dick.

Angelo groaned as he felt his shaft enter the beautiful wetness of Megan's mouth. Jorge's rigorous pounding ensured that Angelo's dick was plunging deeply into Megan's throat, almost to the base of his shaft. The girl was deepthroating him and her eyes were glued on his. Angelo snapped off a few photos from his perspective and then tossed the camera onto the pillows and out of the way so that he could grab Megan by her head with both of his hands and fuck her mouth.

Megan's cries became muffled as she was fucked by two guys at either extremity. Jorge slapped her ass again and Angelo felt the vibration as Megan groaned with cock in her mouth.

They fucked her like that for 5 minutes. And then 10 minutes.

The orgasm built and then erupted. Angelo kept his hands firmly on Megan's head, not allowing her to pull away as he squirted his hot cum down her gorgeous throat.

Jorge suddenly groaned as well and thrust hard against Megan's ass as he finished inside her as well.

They all fell apart from each other and Megan fell limply onto the bed and moaned from the hardcore fucking that she had just received.

"I'm not going to be able to walk down those stairs after that," she said, looking to Jorge's huge cock with affection in her eyes. "I should come here more often," she suggested.

Angelo caught Jorge's masked eye and he laughed.

That didn't sound like a bad idea at all.

Author's Note

This is a work of fiction. Whilst based upon real people, the stories depicted within are the work of the author's imagination and do not represent real events.

Thanks for reading.
Keep an eye out for Volume 2.

Preview

It had been almost three years. Believe me, I was keeping count. Three years since I had last felt a woman underneath me. Sure, there had been a few dates in between that had cost me a small fortune, only to be later rejected. There had even been a handful of young, desperate women that had approached and conspicuously propositioned me on the internet. Invariably, they had been either obese, diseased or ugly beyond description.

I am not an overly vain man, but I do take pride in myself. Were I to sleep with a desperate young woman purely to slake my own desperate lust, then I would feel emasculated and ashamed. I can do better than that.

However, three years had come and gone, and now I had reached the end of my tether. My penis felt more like a cumbersome sloth than the raging bull of my youth. Since the age of sixteen, I had never been more than a few weeks without sex. Now, in my early thirties and since breaking up with my fiancé, the drought was beginning to look like the Sahara.

I considered my options. There was Jessica, the twenty-eight year old television journalist with her sharp mind and her long thighs. We had been on several dates now, all of which had cost me a lot of money and none of which had amounted to anything more than a friendly peck on the cheek and the occasional wink. Then, there was the young girl from the gym who couldn't have been older than twenty, with two kids in the pram and a missing father. She cornered me at the drinking taps as often as she could. She looked as if she were pregnant again, though I suspected that she wasn't. I could never recall her name.

That left me with option number three. This was the option that I had been considering for a few months now and I had finally decided that enough was enough. Am I a man or not? Today was the day.

"Thank you for calling Honey And Silk Escort Service, this is Harmony speaking. What can I do for you today?"

Her voice was astonishing. Soft and breathy.

"Hi, my name is John," I said honestly. "I'm after the most beautiful woman you have for tonight."

"Hi John," Harmony gushed warmly. "Savannah is one of our most beautiful women and she is available to come to you wherever you like. Does that sound to your liking, John?"

I took a deep breath. "Sounds perfect," I said.

"Are you after the girlfriend experience tonight, John?" Harmony continued.

"No," I said firmly, shaking my head as I held the phone to my ear. "Just send her to my room." I gave her the details of the hotel I had chosen for the night.

"That will be eight hundred dollars for tonight, John. How would you like to pay?"

Eight hundred dollars, I mused. I earned more than that in a day. It was no big deal if it meant finally breaking the drought and feeling a woman moving against me again. Hell, the hotel room had cost almost twice that. I gave my credit card details, agreed to a time and hung up the phone. My heart was pounding. It was a combination of nerves and excitement.

I had just booked a prostitute.

I couldn't help wondering what my late mother would've thought if she had found out, but I was quick to dispel the thought. I replaced the image with that of a lion, proudly defending his pride and taking his pick of the harem. A lion did not concern itself with the opinion of the sheep. Nor would I indulge any feelings of guilt about what I was participating in. Life was too short not to enjoy it. Money is nothing - it is artificial. Sex is real. I knew which I valued more.

The room I had booked for the evening came with its own hot tub situated beside a vast, floor to ceiling window that gazed out across the city. There were no buildings higher than us. No prying eyes to look in and witness the debauchery that was planned. There were two bottles of mid-range red wine in a bucket of ice on the table, soft white dressing gowns hanging in the bathroom and chocolates on the pillows.

It was a palace of luxury.

It was how I felt that I deserved to live. Now, all I needed was a luxurious woman to share it with and my life would be complete.

The housing market had stagnated in recent months, but it didn't matter. I had a portfolio of over one hundred investment properties in several countries, effectively insulating me from any localized crashes. That being said, as a general rule, the price of real estate had nowhere to go but up. After all, they stopped making land a long time ago. There was no more precious a commodity and I had aggressively bought up as much of it as I could get my hands on. My days were spent placing phone calls to property managers, playing golf with real estate agents that wanted my money, hitting the gym and then wandering about my empty house at night, wondering why there wasn't a line of women lined up at my front door. I was a catch, after all.

Three years, the voice in my head begged to differ.

Three fuckless years.

I decided not to wait and uncorked the wine. It was a balmy summers afternoon and the pretty weather girl said there was a storm rolling in. The very air had a feeling of anticipation about it. I changed out of the suit and tie and opted instead for a thin shirt and trousers that allowed the breeze to roll through. I decided against wearing underwear, socks or shoes. The open balcony was awash with a heavenly wind that danced around my bare feet as I sipped at the wine and tried to relinquish any inhibitions that I was feeling. *I am alive,* I reminded myself, breathing in the fresh air and the aromas of the wine.

The sun was beginning to set.

There was a TV on the balcony and I found the sports channel. There was a rugby game being played. In fact, if I listened carefully, I could hear the distant roar of the crowd echoing up from the football stadium a few blocks away. If I had brought binoculars or a telescope, I might not have needed the television to watch the game. Rugby was perfect, I decided. Few things could get my testosterone boiling like a rough and tumble game of rugby. The competitive juices were masculine and I indulged myself in the feeling. Anger, decisiveness, strength, lust.

The air began to grow cool as the storm clouds approached and the sinking sun stained the sky in a haunting pink and purple hue.

I heard the doorbell ring.

Somewhere in the distance, lightning flashed and thunder rumbled.

"You must be Savannah," I said, opening the door for my guest.

Savannah extended her hand. "You must be John," she smiled. She brushed past me and entered the room, slipping her hand out of mine and running it across my chest. "This room is just lovely!" she exclaimed.

I closed the door and turned to appraise the prostitute. I was more than impressed. She could've been a model. Her legs flashed from between a slit in her dress as she walked and her hips swayed tantalizingly. She had a shawl across her shoulders which she removed to reveal a perfect pair of breasts hiding under her red dress.

The cumbersome sloth had awoken. I felt like a teenager again.

"Make yourself at home," I said, gesturing with the wine glass. "There's an open bottle on the balcony."

Savannah smiled her seductive smile once again and moved out to the balcony. Together, we leant against the railing and gazed out at the setting sun and the approaching storm clouds.

"What an amazing night," Savannah gushed, closing her eyes and tilting her neck up, allowing the wind to play around her bare neck and cleavage. She wasn't wearing a bra and her nipples were hard. She wore a thin necklace of pearls around her neck and classy earrings to match. Her dark brown hair shone and smelt of roses. I was ready to skip the wine.

It had been three years.

Savannah leant against me and wrapped her arm through mine as we sipped at the wine and enjoyed the alcohol in our bloodstream. I could feel her breasts against my shoulder. I knew in that moment, I had just made the best decision of my life. Suddenly, a whole new world of options had opened up before me and I couldn't wait to dive in and test the water.

I had planned to order room service and have a chat over dinner before getting into it, but Savannah had different ideas and I was all too happy to oblige. She turned her face into my neck and kissed me softly. It felt amazing. She rested her wine glass on the balcony and I took her into my arms, listening to her moan in my ear and delighting in the way she pressed her body against mine. Her dress was silky to the touch and her tanned skin felt almost indistinguishable from the soft fabric.

"I want to feel you inside of me, John," Savannah whispered in my ear.

With that, I closed my eyes and felt her hands moving down my chest as she kissed my neck. My dick was throbbing with anticipation. Longing for her touch.

There it was.

Savannah smiled and slowly knelt in front of me, dragging her chin down my stomach - her hands gently squeezing and caressing my bulging manhood.

She unzipped my fly and then - with the wind swirling across the open balcony, the sound of approaching thunder and the feeling of electricity in the air - Savannah the prostitute guided my dick into the tender warmth and wetness of her mouth.

Three years and now, *finally*, I felt like a man again.

Savannah sucked, licked and kissed my dick delightfully, pulling away occasionally to smile and bat her eyelids up at me whilst her hands continued the work. The woman was masterful at eliciting pleasure.

I enjoyed the experience for a few minutes, reveling in the feeling of her hot breath as her lips wrapped around my hard shaft. The wind blew and I sipped at my wine again, feeling almost overwhelmed with sensual pleasures. I briefly wondered if anyone in the city could see us out here on the balcony but then I dismissed the thought. Let them look, I thought. I hope they enjoy themselves half as much as I am enjoying it.

I pulled Savannah to her feet again and slipped her dress of her shoulders. It fell to the floor to reveal her naked body, still standing in her heels. The woman was a goddess in human form. Perfectly shaped, large breasts, toned stomach and never ending legs.

I pulled my shirt over my head and stepped out of my trousers. The feeling of the warm wind against my naked body felt excruciatingly good. The bull inside of me took charge and I grabbed the prostitute around her waist and lifted her up against the balcony railing. Savannah squealed and laughed as she glanced down at the street, hundreds of meters below. She wrapped her legs around me and, pressed up against the railing, I entered her.

If her mouth had been tender, warm and wet, her pussy felt like something reserved only for gods and kings. It was heaven on Earth and I felt as if I might explode right there inside her. I thrusted slowly at first, listening to her moaning in pleasure as I moved inside of her.

We moved together in rhythm. In the distance, the roar of a crowd cheering signaled a big moment in the rugby game. Lightning flashed and the first patters of rain splashed against our bare skin. We were like insignificant beings floating in an ocean, yet we were utterly consumed with each other and what was transpiring in our shared space.

As the rain got heavier, Savannah wrapped her arms and legs around me and I carried her inside, still thrusting inside of her. I lay her down on the soft carpet and fucked her with purpose. Her perfect breasts bounced deliciously and Savannah threw her head back and moaned in a wild manner that was hugely gratifying whilst I thrust deeply into her. She was feminine in the extreme and, by contrast, I felt like the king of the world as I lay on top of this gorgeous woman and slid my dick in and out of her.

Soon, I was climaxing. I somewhat reluctantly pulled out and, kneeling over Savannah's moaning figure, I finished on her tits.

I was gasping for breath and groaning as I finished and I rolled over and joined her on the carpet. "Wow," I breathed, still feeling the throbbing after effects of the orgasm.

But Savannah wasn't finished.

Smiling, she massaged the hot cum into her skin and knelt over me, pushing her hair back behind her ears. Then, as I continued to throb, she put my dick in her mouth once again and sucked it gently and slowly. It was amazing in the extreme.

"Next time, you can come inside me," Savannah grinned, finally laying back and slipping her heels off her feet with a satisfied groan.

I just laughed as I lay there, spread-eagled and naked on the carpet. I felt like doing nothing else, aside from maybe running out onto the rain soaked balcony and shouting triumphantly across the city.

So, *this* is what it feels like to be a man.

I had almost forgotten.

Savannah hurried out into the pouring rain and collected our sopping wet clothes. I watched her slender figure as she moved, enjoying her beauty. I was taking photographs with my mind, determined to remember this moment and this view of her bending over in the rain for the rest of my life and wishing the night could last that long.

"Uh oh," Savannah laughed as she brought the clothes back inside and plonked them on the table. They were dripping wet. "The rain's really nice and warm," she commented.

"Warm enough to shower in?" I asked, looking at the still sticky liquid on Savannah's breasts.

Savannah smiled and skipped off towards the bathroom. "I'll get some soap," she answered.

I had never felt so relaxed. The carpet was soft and warm and the rain sounded wondrous as it pitter-pattered on the balcony. Lightning flashed and thunder grumbled.

"Come on, lazy!" Savannah exclaimed, bounding back into my line of sight and out into the rain. "Are you gonna join me or what?"

"Joining," I muttered to myself, getting off the floor and strolling out.

"The wine is a little weak," Savannah giggled, sipping at her glass. We had left our wine glasses out in the rain in our haste to get inside and continue fucking.

"There's more where that came from," I assured her.

"Oh, I don't doubt that, sir," Savannah winked cheekily. "We still have all night."

Three long years, I reflected as Savannah soaped her skin and we showered naked in the lukewarm rain. The lights had come on across the city and the view from the high-rise balcony was breath taking. There was still a tinge of pink in the west as the sun lingered beyond the horizon. Three long years.

Never again, I realized. Never again would I go without sex. I had discovered the incredible world of prostitution and I couldn't shake the feeling that this was the first evening of the rest of my life. It was all easy pickings from here. Anything I wanted, I could have it. I had the money and the uneasiness factor had been obliterated. In fact, I found myself wondering why I hadn't tried this years ago.

Printed in Great Britain
by Amazon

26907160R00037